STERLING CHILDREN'S BOOKS
New York

An Imprint of Sterling Publishing Co., Inc.
1166 Avenue of the Americas
New York, NY 10036

ISBN 978-1-4549-2774-7

Distributed in Canada by Sterling Publishing Co., Inc.
c/o Canadian Manda Group, 664 Annette Street
Toronto, Ontario M6S 2C8, Canada
Distributed in the United Kingdom by GMC Distribution Services
Castle Place, 166 High Street, Lewes, East Sussex BN7 1XU, England
Distributed in Australia by NewSouth Books
45 Beach Street, Coogee NSW 2034, Australia

For information about custom editions, special sales, and premium and corporate purchases,
please contact Sterling Special Sales at 800-805-5489 or specialsales@sterlingpublishing.com.

Manufactured in China
Lot #:
2   4   6   8   10   9   7   5   3   1
12/17

sterlingpublishing.com

The artwork for this book was prepared using pencil and acrylic paints.

TIME
for a
TRIP

by Phillis Gershator
illustrated by David Walker

STERLING CHILDREN'S BOOKS
New York

Today's the day!
We need to pack.

Books and blankie,
toys, clothes, snack.

Gifts I made
with sticks and glue.

Bunny says,
"I'm coming, too."

No more room!
My bag won't zip.

What time is it?

Time for a trip!

How will we go?
By bus? By plane?

Chug,
chug,
chug
in a choo-choo train?

By helicopter?
Pony cart?

Scooter for a speedy start?

Row a boat?
Don't let it tip!
What time is it?

Time for a trip!

How will we go?
By ferry? Bike?

Hot air balloon?
That's what I'd like!

Ride a rocket?
Sail a ship?
What time is it?

Time for a trip!

How will we go?
It's not too far.

We're on our way . . .

. . . we'll go by car!

All aboard.
Get ready, set.
Buckle up.
Are we there yet?

The wheels go round.
We roll along.
Look out the window.
Sing a song.

Count the trucks.
Take a nap.

Stop to stretch.

Check the map.

Here we are!
We hop and skip.

We took a trip!
We took a trip!

It's time for hugs
and kisses, too,
and giving gifts.

Thank you!
Thank you!

Gramps and Gram
are glad we came.

We tell a story.
Play a game.

Take a picture.

Read a book.

Pick peas, pull carrots.

Be a cook.

Learn to do
a double flip.

What time is it?

Time for a trip?

But I don't *want* to say good-bye!

Please don't be sad.
Do you know why?

Even though it's time to go
we'll see you soon.
WE LOVE YOU SO!